2464
3.4
.5

W9-BUS-283

Learning to Read, Step by Step!

Ready to Read **Preschool–Kindergarten**
• big type and easy words • rhyme and rhythm • picture clues
For children who know the alphabet and are eager to begin reading.

Reading with Help **Preschool–Grade 1**
• basic vocabulary • short sentences • simple stories
For children who recognize familiar words and sound out new words with help.

Reading on Your Own **Grades 1–3**
• engaging characters • easy-to-follow plots • popular topics
For children who are ready to read on their own.

Reading Paragraphs **Grades 2–3**
• challenging vocabulary • short paragraphs • exciting stories
For newly independent readers who read simple sentences with confidence.

Ready for Chapters **Grades 2–4**
• chapters • longer paragraphs • full-color art
For children who want to take the plunge into chapter books but still like colorful pictures.

STEP INTO READING® is designed to give every child a successful reading experience. The grade levels are only guides. Children can progress through the steps at their own speed, developing confidence in their reading, no matter what their grade.

Remember, a lifetime love of reading starts with a single step!

To my dad
—J.G.

For my parents
—R.N.W.

Text copyright © 1998 by Julie Glass. Illustrations copyright © 1998 by Richard Walz.
All rights reserved under International and Pan-American Copyright
Conventions. Published in the United States by Random House Children's Books,
a division of Random House, Inc., New York, and simultaneously in
Canada by Random House of Canada Limited, Toronto.

www.stepintoreading.com

Educators and librarians, for a variety of teaching tools, visit us at
www.randomhouse.com/teachers

Library of Congress Cataloging-in-Publication Data
Glass, Julie.
The fly on the ceiling / by Julie Glass ; illustrated by Richard Walz.
   p.   cm. — (Step into reading. A step 4 book)
SUMMARY: A story about how the very messy French philosopher René Descartes
invented an ingenious way to keep track of his possessions.
ISBN 0-679-88607-9 (trade) — ISBN 0-679-98607-3 (lib. bdg.)
1. Descartes, René, 1596–1650—Juvenile fiction. [1. Descartes, René, 1596–1650—Fiction.
2. Graphic methods—Fiction.   3. Orderliness—Fiction.]
I. Walz, Richard, ill.   II. Title.   III. Series: Step into reading. Step 4 book.
PZ7.G481235Fl   2004   E—dc22   2003012538

Printed in the United States of America   14 13 12 11

STEP INTO READING, RANDOM HOUSE, and the Random House colophon are
registered trademarks of Random House, Inc.

The Fly on the Ceiling
A Math Reader

By Dr. Julie Glass
Illustrated by Richard Walz

Random House 🏠 New York

This is the story of a guy who lived a long time ago. He lived in France.

He was a French guy, so he had a French name. His name was René Descartes (pronounced ruh-NAY day-CART). This may sound like a funny name to you, but in France it is perfectly normal.

René was a philosopher. A philosopher is someone who thinks about why things are the way they are.

René was a *great* philosopher. Many of his ideas are still famous today.

But even though René was a great philosopher, he did have one problem.

He was messy.

This problem started out small. But it got bigger and bigger!

The funny thing was, René did not know he had a problem until…

…he started to lose things.

His notebook.

His favorite hat.

His book about stars.

His inkwell.

Then he found the inkwell.

Now René knew he had a problem.

"This must stop!" René said to himself.
He decided to take a walk and try to
think of a solution to his problem.

It took him a moment to find his coat,
his hat, and the front door.

René went to his favorite bakery to buy
a fresh loaf of bread.

Then he headed to his favorite place to
think: the banks of the river Seine.

René ate some of the bread while he walked. He looked at the water and wondered how he could keep better track of his things.

Night fell and René was still thinking.
He was thinking so hard that he didn't look
where he was going.

SPLASH!

Into the Seine went René Descartes!

When he was fished out of the water, he
was cold and wet, and his bread was soggy.

René walked home. By the time he got there, he was sneezing and wheezing.

He crawled into bed and fell fast asleep.

The next morning, René still felt
dreadful. Not only that, but he couldn't find
a handkerchief...

or an extra blanket...

or the logs to make a fire.

He couldn't even find his soggy bread,
which should have dried out by then.

René crawled sadly back into bed. He stared at his ceiling. The ceiling was the only place in his room that wasn't messy.

René wished that he lived on the neat ceiling instead of on the messy floor.

Just then, he noticed a fly on the
ceiling. The fly flew off and landed near
one corner.

Then it flew off and landed in another
corner. Then it landed above René's toes.

Then it stopped right over René's head.

René started to think. He wondered if the fly ever landed in the same place twice. This might seem like a weird thing to think about, but René was a philosopher, so it was normal for him.

"I need to record where the fly lands so I can know how many times it lands in the same place," he thought. "But how can I do that?"

René thought and thought. Suddenly,
he had a brilliant idea. It was so brilliant
that he jumped out of bed and did a jig!

He knew how to record *exactly* where
the fly landed on the ceiling!

René took a piece of charcoal from the
fire. Then he climbed up on a chair and
started drawing lines on the ceiling. (Don't
try this at home—your parents won't like
it.)

First René drew lines from the north wall to the south wall.

Next he drew lines from
one side to the other.

Then he numbered
the lines along two of
the walls. After that,
he got back into bed.

2

1

0

1   2   3

René watched the fly on the ceiling. When it landed, he counted the lines *over* to that spot. He wrote down the number of lines: 2.

Then he counted the lines *up* to that spot. He wrote down the number: 5.

Together, the two numbers—2 and 5—told him exactly where the fly was!

The numbers 2 and 5 are called *coordinates*. The first coordinate, 2, measures how far away the fly is from the left side. The second coordinate, 5, measures how far away the fly is from the bottom wall.

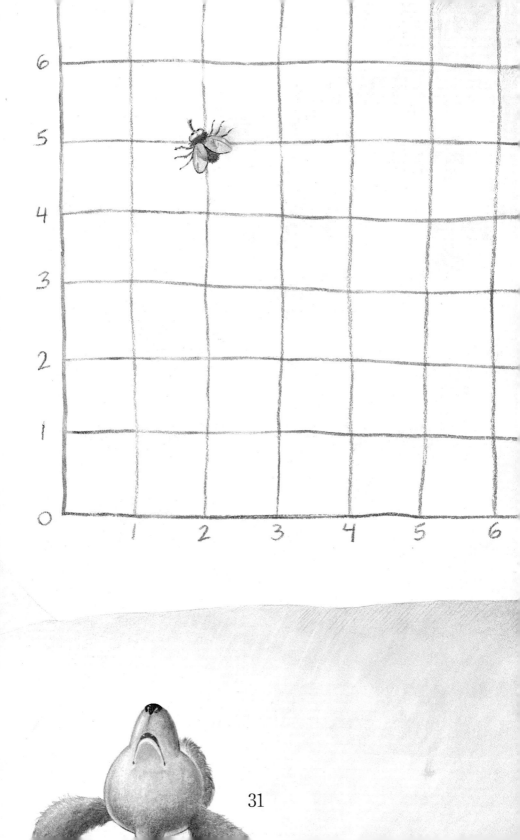

René spent the whole morning watching the fly…and sneezing.

If you had gone to visit him, he might have said, "The fly is six over, three up (6, 3)."

Or "The fly is four over, seven up (4, 7)."

Or "The fly is eight over, one up (8, 1)."

Every spot on the ceiling had its own set of coordinates!

Recording the coordinates of the fly over and over again gave René another brilliant idea.

Maybe he could keep track of his stuff the same way he kept track of the fly! It would be even easier because a hat can't get up and fly away.

René jumped out of bed again. He
pushed everything into the kitchen.

Now the floor of his room was as clean
as his ceiling. But he couldn't draw the
grid on the floor with charcoal—it would
rub off too soon.

René went next door to see if his
neighbor had any paint. What luck! His
neighbor was a painter!

René and the painter painted a grid on René's floor.

Then they went to the bakery to buy
bread.

By the time they got back, the paint
had dried. The painter helped René put his
things in place on the grid.

They found René's hat, his star book, his quill pens, his old boots, his journal from when he was ten, and many other things that René didn't even know were missing.

On a chart, René carefully recorded where everything went.

Voilà!

BOOTS 4,4
STAR BOOK 4,5
CACTUS 3,8
HAT 6,7
JOURNAL 3,
BAGEL
AEOLIPILE 6,4
CHAMBER POT 5,2
INK 1,6
CANDLE
CHEESE

After that, René's home was never
messy again.

Well, hardly ever.

René's system caught on around the world. It was named the *Cartesian* (car-TEE-zhen) *Coordinate System*. ("Cartesian" comes from René's last name: Des*cartes*.)

Today, people still use the Cartesian Coordinate System in many different ways.

Author's Note

Okay, so maybe René Descartes wasn't *really* messy. And maybe he didn't *really* fall into the Seine or draw lines on his ceiling.

But even if nobody knows exactly how he did it, it is a FACT that René Descartes made the Cartesian Coordinate System very popular.

And he was a darn good philosopher, too.